SMARTPHONES
AND SOCIETY

Are Smartphones a Threat to Privacy?

By Carol Kim

ReferencePoint
Press®

San Diego, CA

For more information, contact:
ReferencePoint Press, Inc.
PO Box 27779
San Diego, CA 92198
www.ReferencePointPress.com

LIBRARY OF CONGRESS CATALOGING-IN-PUBLICATION DATA

Names: Kim, Carol, author.
Title: Are smartphones a threat to privacy? / by Carol Kim.
Description: San Diego, CA : ReferencePoint Press, Inc., [2021] | Series: Smartphones and society | Includes bibliographical references and index.
Identifiers: LCCN 2020002706 (print) | LCCN 2020002707 (eBook) | ISBN 9781682829394 (hardcover) | ISBN 9781682829400 (eBook)
Subjects: LCSH: Cell phones and teenagers--Juvenile literature. | Privacy, Right of--Juvenile literature. | Cell phones--Security measures--Juvenile literature. | Smartphones--Social aspects--Juvenile literature.
Classification: LCC HQ799.2.C45 K56 2021 (print) | LCC HQ799.2.C45 (eBook) | DDC 303.48/33--dc23
LC record available at https://lccn.loc.gov/2020002706
LC eBook record available at https://lccn.loc.gov/2020002707

CONTENTS

PRIVACY CHALLENGES IN THE SMARTPHONE AGE

Math teacher Lisa Magrin's day began at 7:00 a.m. when she traveled 14 miles (23 km) to the middle school where she works. At the end of her workday, she attended a Weight Watchers meeting. Then she drove to a doctor's office. Later she went to a park to walk her dog.

Magrin did not provide this information to the *New York Times*. Yet *New York Times* reporters were able to accurately recount to her exactly where she had gone and for how long throughout the day. With Magrin's permission, the reporters had reviewed a database of information from a company that received tracking information collected

Many people rely on their smartphones for directions. Global positioning system (GPS) apps gather users' location data for accurate results.

from her smartphone. By analyzing the tracking data, the reporters were able to piece together her day with amazing accuracy. They shared their findings in a 2018 article about smartphones and data privacy.

The amount and type of information that is collected and shared from smartphones causes many people to worry that their privacy is at risk. Magrin found the tracking of her day disturbing. "It's the thought of people finding out those intimate details that you don't want [them] to know," she said.[1]

SMARTPHONES AND PRIVACY

Today, more than 2.5 billion people worldwide own a smartphone. A smartphone is a handheld cellular phone that is capable of performing many of the functions of a computer. Besides providing phone service, smartphones connect to the internet, making web browsing and email always accessible. Other smartphone functions include texting and global positioning system (GPS) navigation.

Smartphones became popular in the 2010s. David Choffnes is an associate professor at Northeastern University's Khoury College of Computer Sciences. He says, "When smartphones first came out, we were so excited for the new services that we didn't really think about privacy; we hadn't had something like a smartphone before, so we didn't think of the implications."[2] However, as smartphones became important fixtures in

Many fitness apps, such as Strava, access GPS data. They use location data to determine a user's route and the distance the user traveled.

people's lives, concerns about users' privacy began to emerge. Many smartphone users want to know how much of their personal data is extracted and shared from their phones. Another concern is how the data is used.

When people go online, they often share some of their personal lives with the world. For example, in order to make an online purchase, buyers need to provide

More than 200 million Americans shop online, and many also do online banking. They may share their credit card and banking account information.

their credit card number. They usually also need to share their email address for communications and their home mailing address so their purchase can be shipped to them. Each piece of information by itself may not appear to pose much risk to a person's privacy. However, the information accumulates. Lorraine Courtney is a journalist who writes for the newspaper the *Irish Independent*. She explains, "When tiny bits of information are incessantly given to an ever-consuming, ever-calculating algorithm, they add up to a shockingly complete picture of us."[3]

Public awareness of smartphone privacy issues has been growing. By learning about data collection and how it affects both individuals and societies, people can better understand smartphone privacy concerns. Then they can take steps to protect their privacy. Facebook founder and chief executive officer (CEO) Mark Zuckerberg has declared, "The future is private."[4] Whether or not that is true remains to be seen.

CHAPTER ONE

WHAT ARE THE PRIVACY CONCERNS REGARDING SMARTPHONES?

Personal data has become one of the most valuable and sought-after resources in the world. People routinely give up their personal data without understanding how much they are revealing, who it is given to, and how much it is worth. The management consulting firm McKinsey Global Institute estimates that the business of collecting, analyzing, and selling data is a $300 billion a year industry. Jesse Leimgruber is the cofounder of the data technology company Bloom. He says that in the United States alone, "more than 10,000 companies are pooling and selling your personal data."[5]

Many people use their phones for entertainment purposes when they are bored or to pass the time while waiting. They may be sharing personal data without realizing it.

Most personal data is collected from people's online activities, which largely take place on computers and smartphones. Because smartphones have become an increasingly fundamental part of people's everyday lives, they play a key role in modern privacy concerns. Smartphones and other devices have the potential to make users' lives less private.

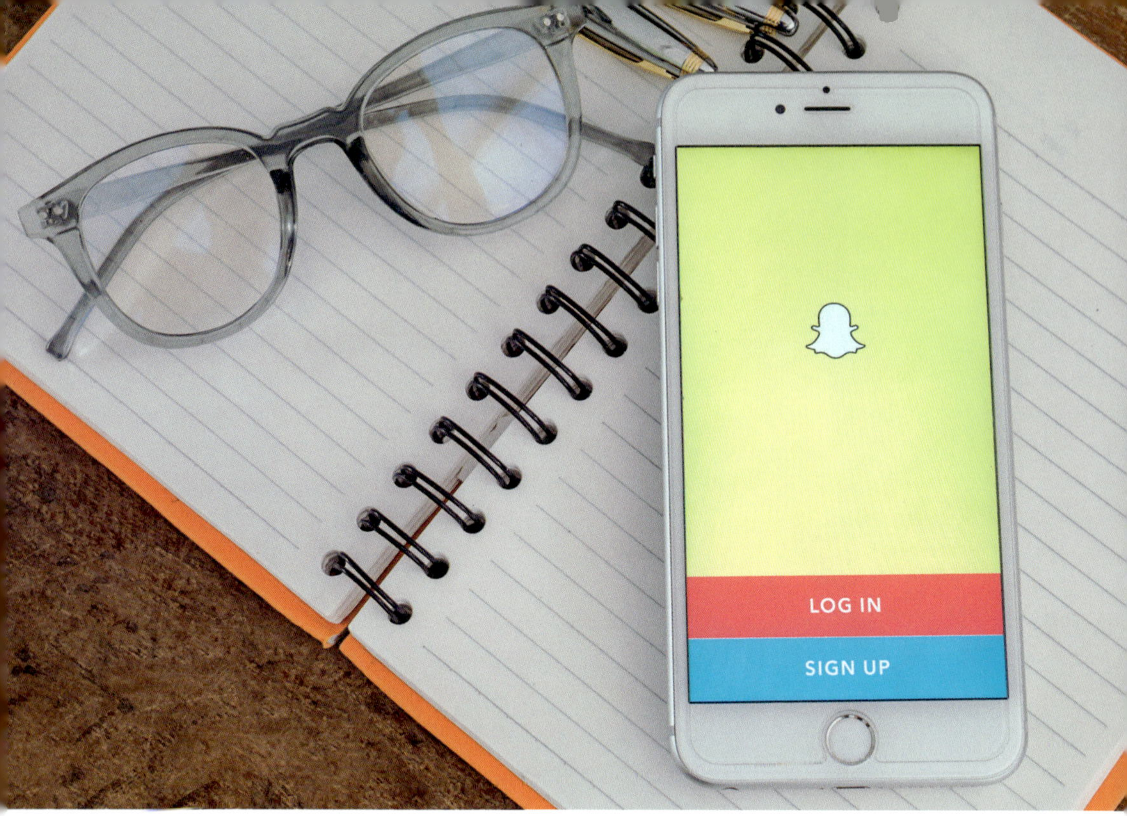

Snapchat was created in 2011. Since then, it has become one of the most popular social media platforms.

THE EVOLUTION OF SMARTPHONES

Cell phones have been around since the 1970s, although those early models bear little resemblance to the cell phones of today. The technology company International Business Machines (IBM) introduced the first phone with smart features in 1992. It was called the Simon Personal Communicator. It had some computer-like functions, such as the ability to send and receive emails. It had a touchscreen and came loaded with a calendar, calculator, clock, map program, news display, and more. Then, in 2007, the technology company Apple introduced the first iPhone. The era of the modern smartphone began. Apple CEO Steve Jobs called the iPhone a "revolutionary device . . . that changes everything."[6]

Today's smartphones are able to run a variety of software programs called applications, or apps. Mobile apps have many functions. Some are practical tools, such as navigation or note-taking apps. Others provide information, such as weather or sports apps. Many apps provide entertainment, such as game or music-playing apps. Social media apps such as Twitter, Instagram, and Snapchat are also hugely popular.

DEFINING THE PRIVACY ISSUE

Many authorities in the technology field have a dim view of modern society's ability to protect people's privacy. Harvard University computer science professor Margo Seltzer declared, "Privacy as we knew it in the past is no longer feasible. . . . How we conventionally think of privacy is dead."[7] When people use smartphone apps, they give up some privacy. For example, people may use apps to help them find a restaurant, check the traffic, buy a textbook, or schedule a medical appointment.

The apps collect users' location information, food preferences, buying habits, and even sensitive health care information. The apps' developers can sell this data to companies. Companies can use the data to help them market their products to people.

Some people try to break into smartphones. These hackers may get through a phone's security features. Then they can steal people's personal data. Ed Cabrera is the chief cybersecurity officer at TrendMicro, a digital security company. He helps people protect their data. He says, "Apps may request administrative privileges to your data, and those privileges could be used by the app later on, or by some malware, to steal your personal information."[8] Malware is a type of software that infects people's devices. Hackers often use malware to steal personal information.

Hackers use personal information in different ways. Some sell the data through the dark web to make a profit. The dark web is a secret part of the internet that is difficult to access. Other hackers use the data to steal a person's identity. They may set up false credit card accounts in the person's name or use the information to access the person's bank accounts. Then they can steal money from the person. Using a person's identity for financial gain and

IDENTITY THEFT AND FRAUD BY THE NUMBERS

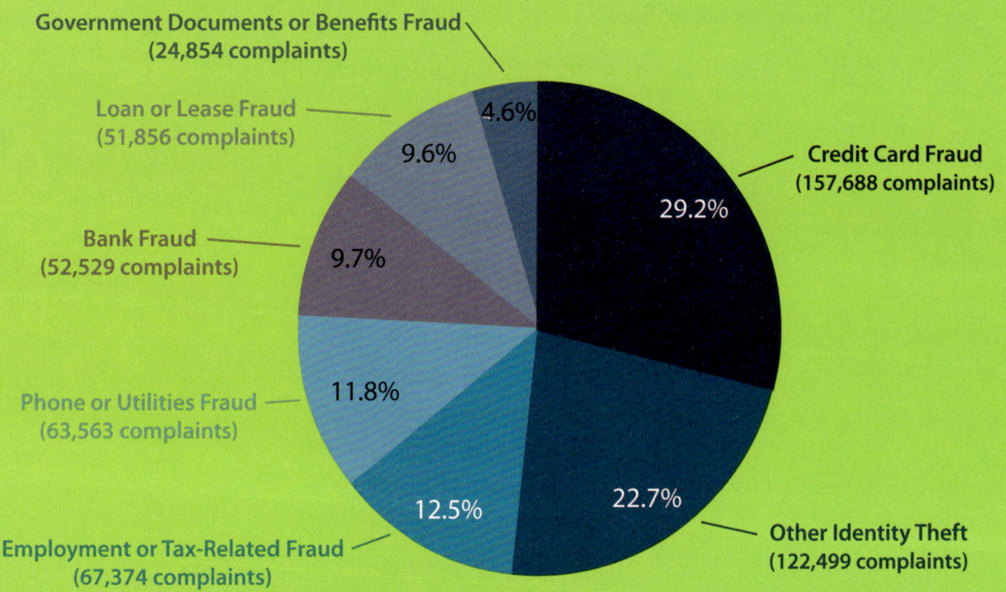

In 2018, the Federal Trade Commission received more than 500,000 reports of identity theft and identity fraud. This graph breaks down the complaints by category and percentage.

"Consumer Sentinel Network Data Book 2018," Federal Trade Commission, *February 2019. www.ftc.gov.*

other benefits is called identity fraud. Identity theft and identity fraud are common.

Tech companies such as Apple and Google try to vet apps that are sold from their app stores. However, they cannot guarantee a user's data will be protected. Many apps require access to certain types of data. Reputable app developers will ask users to grant permission to access this data when the app is downloaded. But not all app developers do this. Shelby Brown is a reporter who writes for the technology website CNET. She says, "Researchers discovered that over 1,000 apps that 'bent the rules' have horned in on your privacy, even when you told them not to."[9]

Because so many people own and use smartphones, personal data collection is widespread. In 2019, the Pew Research Center estimated that 81 percent of US adults owned a smartphone. This number is even higher among US teens. In 2018, Pew estimated that 95 percent of US teens own or have access to a smartphone. Many people who own smartphones use them every day. Based on the results of a 2018 survey, Pew estimated that 28 percent of all US adults and 45 percent of all US teens were online almost constantly.

WHY IS PRIVACY A SMARTPHONE ISSUE?

Changes in smartphone technology occur at a rapid pace. The technology is constantly updated. This makes it difficult to keep up with the latest privacy threats. David Ellis teaches media and communication studies at York University in Toronto. He says, "Much like a mutating virus, digital services and devices keep churning out new threats along with the new benefits—making mitigation efforts a daunting and open-ended challenge for everyone."[10]

Because smartphones are essentially handheld computers, they carry with them additional privacy concerns not found with non-mobile devices. With technological advances, there is little people can do on a desktop computer or laptop that they cannot also do on a smartphone. As a result, more and more people rely only on their smartphones to get online.

Some people have smart watches, a type of wearable device that has apps like a smartphone. Smart watches store data and can be used for everyday activities such as making a payment.

Unlike a computer or even a tablet, cell phones have become people's constant companions. Most smartphone users keep their phones nearby at all times. Smartphones log information not gathered by a computer or tablet, such as calls, text messages, and location data. In addition, thanks to their sensors and connected devices, smartphones can record physical information. They can detect motion, log a user's heart rate, and record how many steps the user has taken in a day. They may also store information about a user's fingerprints and facial features.

WHO ARE THE PLAYERS INVOLVED?

The issue of smartphone privacy involves many different players. Each has a role in addressing how best to provide privacy protections. Manufacturing companies make the smartphone's hardware. Some of the major manufacturers include Samsung, Apple, and LG Electronics. These companies load the phones with various sensors, such as fingerprint and facial recognition sensors. The sensors allow the phone to recognize a user's fingerprints and facial features. These are security tools. The phone will only unlock if the data matches.

Then there are the companies that make a phone's operating system. An operating system is the software that allows a phone to carry out functions and run apps. The main operating systems are Android and iOS. Google makes the Android operating system, and Apple makes iOS.

Another important player is the service provider. In the United States, the biggest service providers are AT&T, Verizon, Sprint, and T-Mobile. Service providers build the cell phone towers that send signals so people can make calls on their phones. They collect data on people's phone use history.

App developers also collect certain data from people's phones. This category is huge. Many companies and people create apps. In May 2019, the media company Business of Apps reported that users could choose from 2.6 million Android apps and 2.2 million iOS apps.

Location data companies play a role in data collection too. Most of these companies are not widely known to the public. These companies provide app developers with a location-tracking feature that can be incorporated into their apps. Currently, more than 1,000 apps contain these location-tracking features. In 2019, the location data company Foursquare estimated that 10 million Americans had downloaded an app that had a location-tracking feature. *Fast Company* magazine editor Katharine Schwab wrote, "You might be included in this dataset and have no idea."[11]

Each of these players has a different way of earning money from their products. Apple is mainly a hardware manufacturer that makes smartphones and other devices, along with the operating systems that run on them. It earns money from the sale of these devices. Google also makes smartphones and other devices. But its focus is on data, and it mostly makes money from advertising. For this reason, Google collects a lot of data from its users.

Verizon is one of the most popular choices for cell phone service. In 2019, Verizon's 4G network covered 70 percent of the United States.

App developers also rely heavily on data collection as a source of revenue. Many make their products available for free to users. But the cost for the app is essentially paid in the form of information provided by the user. This data is valuable, especially when it comes to advertising.

Despite the role other parties play in data collection, smartphone users themselves are the most important players. How people choose to use their smartphones has a huge impact on their privacy. In a 2016 survey, the Pew Research Center found that US smartphone owners varied widely in their privacy practices. Pew researchers estimated that 22 percent of these people used all of the standard privacy protections, such as a screen lock and regular updates to the phone's operating system and apps. The researchers found that 28 percent of US smartphone owners did not even use screen-locking features.

WHAT HAPPENS TO THE DATA?

When manufacturers create smartphones, they must decide what kind of sensors to include in the phones. This affects the kinds of data that will be collected. Operating system and app developers decide how that data will be protected and how it will be distributed. They decide how much control users will have over their data. Some data, such as photos and email contacts, is stored directly on the device. But other data, such as a user's location information and web browsing history, is sent to other companies. The information is sent over a Wi-Fi or cellular network. While data may be protected during this transmission phase, this is not always the case. The data is stored on the company's storage system, sometimes referred to as the cloud. The data can then be copied and shared. Often it travels far beyond where it was originally collected. It can be sent to the US government or to companies that analyze the data. The data analytics companies can then sell the data to advertisers or app developers. Advertisers use this information to develop targeted ads. Targeted ads are designed to appeal to a certain group of people.

App developers can use this information to develop new apps targeted to specific users.

WHAT PRIVACY PROTECTIONS EXIST?

The responsibility to protect the privacy of smartphone users falls to all the players involved. This includes the device manufacturers and the operating system developers. Google, Apple, Facebook, and other technology companies have a huge role in influencing how well information can be protected.

App developers, service providers, smartphone users, and the government also have a responsibility to make

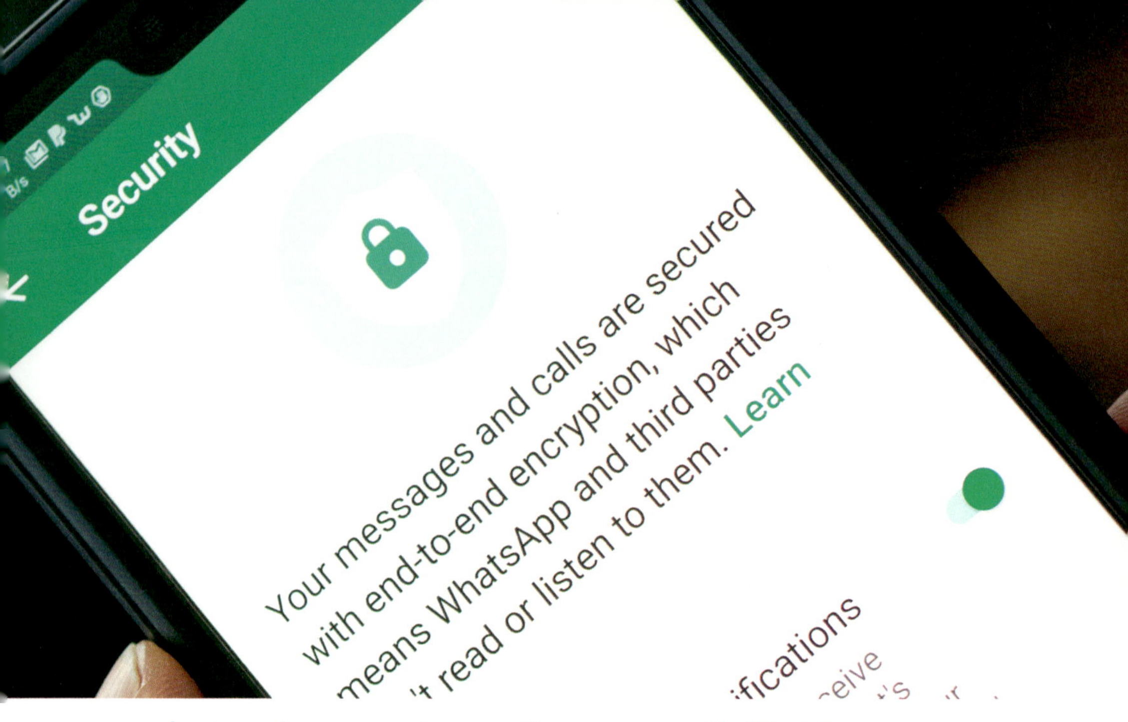

Apps may have separate encryption processes. On WhatsApp, messages are encrypted, making it extremely difficult for those outside the conversation to access the content.

sure the privacy of users is protected. How well each player succeeds varies widely. For example, when choosing to download an app to their phone, users must give permission for the app to access certain types of data. Some app developers are clear about what kind of data is requested and how it may be used. But sometimes they gather unrelated data that is not needed for the app. Once the smartphone user gives the app permission to collect data, the app's developers can send the data to anyone they choose, and they do not need to reveal this to the user.

People can use special tools to protect their smartphone data. These tools include encryption and sandboxing.

Encryption makes data unreadable by anyone unless they have a key. The key is usually a passcode or another identification tool that unlocks the data, or makes it readable. On iPhones, users' data is automatically encrypted once they set up a passcode. This is also the case with some Android phones. Users can also set up encryption manually on their smartphones. Many smartphones have an "Encrypt phone" option in their settings. Selecting this option encrypts the user's data.

Sandboxing is another data protection tool that can be found on iPhones and Android phones. This security measure keeps information collected by one app from being accessed by another. If a virus or malware infects one app on a person's phone, sandboxing prevents the virus or software from spreading further. A virus is a computer program that tries to replicate itself and spread so it infects other devices.

The public, the government, and technology companies are becoming increasingly aware of the privacy concerns surrounding smartphone use. People have studied this topic extensively and have attempted to address the privacy threats that have emerged. Yet despite these efforts, smartphone privacy continues to be a major issue.

CHAPTER TWO

HOW DOES SMARTPHONE PRIVACY AFFECT INDIVIDUALS?

When asked, many Americans say they care about protecting their privacy and personal data. In a 2019 Pew Research Center survey of Americans, 79 percent of the respondents reported being concerned about how their data was being used by companies. Sixty-four percent of the respondents worried about how the government might be using their data. Still, many users do not take even the most basic steps to protect their smartphone data. Researchers refer to the common practice of caring about privacy while still allowing a lot of personal data to be released as the "privacy paradox." Many people want greater data privacy, but their behavior makes it appear

as if they do not think it matters. Giovanni Buttarelli, the former data protection supervisor for the European Union (EU), explained the complexity of the privacy paradox: "The so-called Privacy Paradox is not that people have conflicting desires to hide and to expose. The paradox is that we have not yet learned how to navigate the new possibilities and vulnerabilities opened up by rapid digitization."[12]

The law does not require apps to have terms of service agreements, but many apps have these agreements. When users download the apps, they must to agree to these terms. A terms of service agreement explains the type of data the app will collect, and it asks the user to give permission to access this data. However, many users accept the agreement without reading through it fully. They may simply scroll through and click the "accept" button at the bottom of the agreement.

Also, many app developers do not make their terms of service agreements clear and easy to read. These agreements are often long and include technical language that many users may not understand. Researchers estimate it would take one person seventy-six hours to read through all of the terms of service agreements he or she encounters in a year. David Hoffman is a professor at the University of Pennsylvania Law School. He says, "There's a real concern that consumer protection law is basically being swallowed by click-by-agree clauses."[13]

Smartphone users may have many reasons for not taking steps to better protect their data. Many users believe the benefits of sharing personal data outweigh the risks. The disclosure of personal information is a price they are willing to pay in exchange for free apps and services. Some users may be in denial. They think the risks of data sharing only apply to others, not to themselves.

PHONE SENSORS

One way that smartphone user data is collected is through sensors. These sensors gather information about a phone's movement and the surrounding environment in real time. There are many types of smartphone sensors. Some of the most common sensors are accelerometers, gyroscopes, and magnetometers. Accelerometers measure where a phone is pointing and how fast it is moving. Gyroscopes track small motions or movements. When paired with

Some smartphones have sensors that can track a person's heart rate and steps. People can use these features to monitor their exercise.

accelerometers, gyroscopes can measure a user's steps and movement. Gyroscopes also help users take panoramic photos and are useful for some game apps. Magnetometers are used in map and compass apps. They can determine which way is north.

While these sensors may not appear to pose much of a security risk, they can reveal more than most people would prefer. Maryam Mehrnezhad is a computer scientist who works at Newcastle University in England. She says,

"Sensors are finding their ways into every corner of our lives."[14]

Some sensors are not permission-protected. Any apps that smartphone users install on their phones can access the sensors without the users' permission. Websites visited through smartphone browsers can also access many device sensors without notifying the user or asking for permission. In 2018, a team of researchers studied 100,000 popular websites. They found that nearly 4,000 of these sites were accessing smartphone sensors. While most sites used the sensor data for legitimate purposes, such as orienting pages based on the phone's position, some sites used the data to track or identify users. Nikita Borisov was one of the researchers involved in this study. He is a professor of electrical and computer engineering at the University of Illinois at Urbana-Champaign. He says, "I did not expect that we would find thousands of sites and hundreds of domains that are engaged in using these sensors."[15]

GEOTRACKING

The ability to identify a smartphone's location is called geotracking. Geotracking is often done through the GPS chip embedded in a smartphone. Smartphones also send radio signals to nearby cell towers. These radio signals can be used to calculate a phone's location within about one city block. Service providers have access to this data. Some service providers sell this data to companies.

Most smartphone users routinely give apps permission to track their phone's location. In many cases, geotracking is beneficial for users. Users can get help with navigation or find places such as the closest gas station. However, apps may sell a user's location data to third parties. The user may not want this data to be shared with these other parties.

DATA THEFT AND WI-FI TRACKING

Many smartphone users are quick to tap into a business's free Wi-Fi connection. Coffee shops, department stores, and many other businesses offer free Wi-Fi to customers. Customers enjoy the convenience the free Wi-Fi offers. They do not have to use up their own cell phone data when they plug into Wi-Fi. However, the networks may be unsecured, or not protected by a password. Then users may be more vulnerable to hackers. J.D. Biersdorfer writes technology advice columns for the *New York Times*. She explains, "That free Wi-Fi network may not be so free if it is unsecured and someone hijacks your data."[16] If a network is unsecured, hackers could steal any information people send over the network, including passwords, credit card information, or bank information.

Also, some businesses that offer free Wi-Fi track the online activity of users who log into their Wi-Fi networks. The Wi-Fi connection can provide a store with information about a shopper's behavior while the person is inside the store. Retailers can see how long someone spends in certain parts of the store or what websites he or she may have visited. This information can be used to help retailers send targeted ads or determine how many salespeople to keep on the floor at different times.

Increasingly, stores have moved to collecting location data that is more precise than what can be gathered from GPS or Wi-Fi signals. Smartphones have Bluetooth antennas, which are used to wirelessly connect the phone to accessories such as earphones. Many stores have Bluetooth beacons that allow them to track a shopper's location while the shopper is in the store. Bluetooth beacons can be hidden throughout a store. These radio transmitters can communicate with phone apps. Once an app detects a signal from a beacon, the beacon can send ads targeted to where the user is located within the store. For example, someone who is standing near a display of jewelry may get a targeted ad about rings.

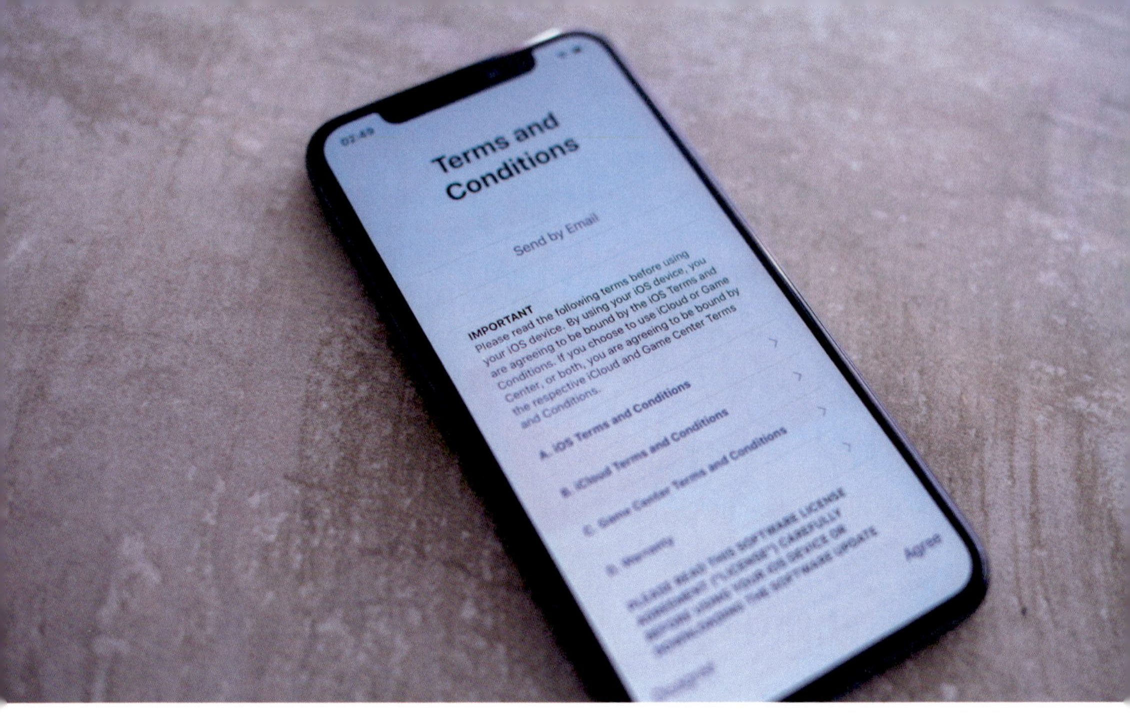

There may be terms and conditions for certain smartphone features, such as the phone's operating system, that the user must agree to. Users often do not carefully read these agreements before signing.

SMARTPHONE APPS

The number of functions a smartphone can provide is greatly increased by installing apps. Once an app is installed and the user agrees to the terms of service, the app's developer can share the user's personal information with any third party. In 2017, a group of academic researchers studied smartphone apps and data collection. They found that more than 70 percent of smartphone apps were sending personal data to third-party tracking companies such as Google and Facebook.

In addition, there have been cases where apps breached users' privacy and shared their data without their permission. In 2019, researchers at the International Computer Science Institute tested 88,000 smartphone apps on the Google Play Store. The Google Play Store is the app store on Android phones. The researchers found that more than 1,300 of these apps were gathering certain personal data even in cases where a user explicitly denied access to the information.

MALICIOUS APPS

Another serious threat to privacy comes from apps that are designed to be harmful. These are called malicious apps. Some of these apps contain viruses or malware. Both viruses and malware interfere with the operation of a device or cause problems for the user. Other types of malicious apps steal private data such as messages, photos, or passwords from the user's phone. Malicious apps may be able to tap into sensors, including the phone's microphone, camera, or GPS. Then the apps can monitor the user's environment or record information, all unbeknownst to the user.

Malicious apps are widespread. In 2019, the mobile security firm Wandera and the computer security company ESET found 172 harmful apps on the Google Play Store. By the time these apps were discovered, they had been installed more than 335 million times.

Android phones have been hit the hardest by malicious apps, largely because Apple has better protections in place than Google does. Apps for iPhones can only be purchased through the official App Store, and fake apps have difficulty gaining access to this marketplace. Apple also makes sure iOS apps cannot gain access to data from other apps or get into the smartphone's operating system.

HOW IS PERSONAL DATA USED?

Many companies, including app developers, social media companies, and credit card companies, send vast amounts of data to other companies called data brokers. Data brokers collect and combine billions of pieces of data and analyze them to learn about common behavioral patterns, usually related to purchasing habits. Data brokers then sell this information to other companies. Companies can use the information to develop targeted ads, which typically results in more people buying their products. These companies often argue that being able to send individuals more relevant ads improves their buying experiences and makes shopping more convenient.

Some data brokers are credit reporting agencies (CRAs). They may share data with people's employers, credit companies, or insurance companies. Privacy analyst Sarah Downey says,

Under the Fair Credit Reporting Act, people have the right to access data that CRAs collect about them.

Data brokers can make conclusions about a person's life based on an analysis of the person's data. For example, they can determine someone's ethnicity, income, educational background,

and marital status. They can also learn about the person's family. The compiled data could even be used to determine private behaviors or details about a person's life in a way that is disadvantageous to them. For example, a smartphone app that tracks a person's activity level could show that she is not very active. The app may share this information with her health insurance company. The health insurance company may then conclude that she does not

Companies can take advantage of cell phone data and browsing history. They can use this information to send targeted ads to a device.

live a healthy lifestyle and decide to raise the cost of her insurance policy.

INEQUALITY AND PRIVACY RISKS

One ongoing trend is the rising number of people who use smartphones as their main method of accessing the internet. In 2019, the Pew Research Center surveyed Americans about their smartphone use. Based on the results of this survey, the researchers estimated that 37 percent of US adults mostly used smartphones to go online, up from 19 percent in 2013.

The Pew study also found that a growing number of people rely solely upon their smartphones to access the internet. They do not have broadband internet service at home. These "smartphone-only" internet users tend to be younger, have a high school education at most, and fall into lower income brackets. Smartphones collect more personal data than other devices do. Also, laptop and desktop computers usually have better security protections than smartphones. Because people bring their smartphones with them nearly everywhere they go, there are more opportunities to collect data from them, especially location information.

People in low income brackets may also only be able to afford inexpensive smartphones. Cheaper phones may have fewer security measures and protections than more expensive, higher-quality phones. *Fast Company* magazine writer Michael Grothaus explains,

> *Economically disadvantaged people often can't afford a luxury like a high-end iPhone or an Android . . . with better privacy protections. As a result, tens of millions of Americans and billions of other people across the world have little choice but to sacrifice their privacy and security if they want to get online, which is a virtual necessity in today's world.*[18]

CHAPTER THREE

HOW DOES SMARTPHONE PRIVACY AFFECT SOCIETIES?

On an individual level, there are clear risks to allowing private data to be released to outside parties. This is especially true when it is not clear who is receiving the data and how it is being used. On a larger level, the accessibility of personal data can pose a threat to entire communities. The government and federal law enforcement can observe large populations of people and collect their personal data. Many people are raising concerns about this widespread surveillance and data collection. Some groups and organizations advocate for stronger data protection laws. They argue that privacy is a human right that all people should have, and that extends to data privacy.

Government agencies such as the National Security Agency may study personal data to identify potential threats to the country. After terrorist attacks in the United States on September 11, 2001, government surveillance increased.

GOVERNMENT SURVEILLANCE

In 2013, cybersecurity expert Edward Snowden was working for the National Security Agency (NSA). The NSA is a US government agency that helps protect the United States from security threats. Snowden found evidence that the NSA was illegally spying on Americans. He leaked classified documents that revealed the NSA's efforts to tap people's cell phones and internet communications. The NSA had ordered Verizon to turn over all of its call records from a three-month period. The NSA had gathered data from millions of phone users, even those who were not criminal suspects. The data included the dates and times people made calls, the phone numbers they called, and how long each phone call lasted. After Snowden leaked this evidence, many cell phone users became more concerned about government surveillance and data privacy.

Then, in 2017, the organization WikiLeaks released documents that appeared to reveal secret cyber tools used by the US Central Intelligence Agency (CIA). Like the NSA, the CIA's goal is to protect and defend the United States. The CIA had used these tools to gather data from people in the United States and around the world. They gathered this data through people's smartphones, televisions, and computers. This revelation also made many people more wary and concerned about their data privacy. According

SURVEILLANCE IN CHINA

While many Americans object to having their personal data collected, a much higher degree of surveillance exists in some other countries. For example, China's government put in place an extensive surveillance system that can track every citizen. Facial recognition equipment on streets can identify individual people within massive crowds. Police can run the image of a person's face through a database to determine the person's identity. When people break even a minor law, such as crossing a street illegally, the police can easily find out who they are. The Chinese government also infringes on citizens' privacy in many ways. Chinese technology companies are required to share their data with the government when asked. The government has even forced Uighurs, an ethnic minority in China, to download an app on their phones that allows the government to gather all of their phone's data.

to the nonprofit organization the American Civil Liberties Union, the US government's surveillance programs have access to most of the communications technologies in use today.

GOVERNMENT PRIVACY PROTECTIONS

The US Supreme Court has cited several constitutional amendments to defend people's right to privacy. One is the Fourth Amendment, which prohibits the police and government from conducting unreasonable searches and seizures of property. A person's cell phone data may be considered personal property. Nevertheless, the United States does not have a broad, comprehensive federal law that protects people's data privacy. Maureen Mahoney is a policy analyst. She says, "There are shockingly few legal privacy protections in the United States."[19] However, there are a few federal laws that provide some targeted protections for individuals. Some states have also adopted privacy laws for their residents to address the need for more protection. In addition, the US Congress is considering a bill called the Geolocation Privacy and Surveillance Act. If this bill is passed, it would better limit how and when a person's location data can be accessed and used. Businesses would not be able to give out a customer's location data without the person's permission. Also, the government would need a probable cause warrant to obtain this data.

A warrant is a document granted by a government official that gives permission to do something. Probable cause means that there is sufficient reason or evidence that someone has committed a crime.

The federal data privacy protection laws currently in place include the Federal Trade Commission (FTC) Act, the Health Insurance Portability and Accountability Act of 1996 (HIPAA), and the Children's Online Privacy Protection Act (COPPA). None of these bills were created with smartphones in mind, but their protections can be extended to today's technology. The FTC Act was passed in 1914. It prohibits "unfair or deceptive" business practices, which includes misleading statements about how companies handle data.[20] The act requires businesses to make privacy policies and user agreements available to all customers. But as long as businesses adhere to these rules, they are mostly free to collect and use personal information as they choose.

HIPAA was passed in 1996. It protects people's medical data. It limits what health care providers can do with

this information. Health care providers cannot disclose
or share someone's medical information without the
person's permission.

The most recent of the three privacy laws is COPPA.
It was passed in 2000. It seeks to place more controls over
how websites, apps, and other online services gather data
from children who are younger than thirteen years old. The
online services must notify a child's parents and obtain
their consent before the child's personal information can
be collected.

Some US states have passed laws to address the
need for privacy legislation. California, Delaware, Utah, and
Illinois have adopted the strictest privacy protection laws.
In 2018, the California Consumer Privacy Act (CCPA) was
passed. It took effect on January 1, 2020. The CCPA put
into place the strictest privacy regulations in the country.
The law gives consumers in California the right to know
what personal data is collected by companies, the reasons
why it is collected, and with whom it is shared. The law also
gives consumers the right to tell companies to delete their
information and not sell it. However, some people think the
law places greater accountability on individuals than on
companies. They think more needs to be done to regulate
companies' data collection practices.

LAW ENFORCEMENT

Law enforcement officials can access personal data from cell phones in special circumstances, such as when a person is suspected of a crime. Some people have raised concerns about how much information law enforcement can access. In 2016, a significant privacy case arose over law enforcement's interest in extracting information from an individual's smartphone. The dispute was between Apple and the Federal Bureau of Investigation (FBI). It involved an iPhone that had belonged to Syed Farook, who was responsible for a December 2015 shooting in San Bernardino, California, in which fourteen people were killed. Farook's phone, which was found by police, was locked by a passcode. When the FBI requested Apple's help to unlock the phone, Apple refused.

The FBI needed Apple's assistance because the company had introduced an encryption feature into the iPhone operating system in 2014. The update made it impossible for anyone without the code, including Apple, to unlock an iPhone. Before 2014, investigators were able to send devices to Apple headquarters with a search warrant in order to gain access.

The FBI sued Apple to try to make the company develop a way to access the data. But Apple refused to cooperate,

People created a memorial to remember the victims of the San Bernardino shooting. Apple refused to help the FBI unlock the shooter's phone over privacy concerns.

citing privacy concerns. Apple CEO Tim Cook said, "The implications of the government's demands are chilling."[21] Apple could have written software to access encrypted phone data, but the company was concerned about the consequences. Cook explained that this software would be "a master key, capable of opening hundreds of millions of locks."[22] In other words, if the FBI could gain access to one iPhone, it could do the same for many other phones. Eventually, the government dropped the court case when it was able to unlock the phone without Apple's help. But the debate between data privacy advocates and those who support greater data access for law enforcement continues.

The Supreme Court is the highest court in the United States. It is part of the judicial branch of the US government.

A HISTORIC RULING

In 2018, the Supreme Court ruled in *Carpenter v. United States* that the government cannot access a person's cell phone location history without a warrant. In the Supreme Court case, Timothy Carpenter was convicted for his involvement in a string of robberies. He helped rob Radio Shack and T-Mobile stores. The FBI obtained a court order. A court order is an order from a judge that gives permission to do something. It requires less evidence that a person is a criminal suspect than a warrant does. It is therefore easier to get a court order than it is to get a warrant. Then the FBI accessed Carpenter's cell phone location data from the cellular service providers MetroPCS and Sprint. The location evidence was used to convict Carpenter.

Orin Kerr is a professor at the University of California, Berkeley, School of Law. He wrote about the case. He said, "It's not an exaggeration to say that the future of surveillance law hinges on how the Supreme Court rules in the case."[23]

The Supreme Court determined that the obtaining of this location data met the definition of a search under the Fourth Amendment and thus required a warrant from a judge. As Chief Justice John Roberts explained, the government had "invaded Carpenter's reasonable expectation of privacy in the whole of his physical movements."[24]

THE CONSEQUENCES OF DATA COLLECTION

Personal data can be used to influence people's actions. This can have wide-reaching consequences that affect entire societies. For example, Donald Trump and his team used data collection to sway voters in the 2016 presidential campaign. The team hired political data firm Cambridge Analytica to help achieve this goal. Cambridge Analytica collected data from as many as 87 million Facebook users without their knowledge or consent. The data was obtained from a quiz app that many Facebook users downloaded.

The app also collected personal information from the users' friends. The information included people's identities, friend networks, and their opinions or preferences based on the things they "liked" on Facebook. Cambridge Analytica used special algorithms and models to find and target millions of US voters who seemed like they could be persuaded to vote for Trump in the election. Then Cambridge Analytica tried to convince them to vote for Trump. It sent targeted political ads on hot-button issues such as gun ownership rights and immigration to potential voters, making them more likely to go to the polls and vote for Trump. Many people believe this strategy significantly affected the outcome of the election.

The FTC launched an investigation into Facebook after the Cambridge Analytica scandal came to light in 2018. Then, in 2019, Facebook agreed to pay a $5 billion fine in a settlement with the FTC for violating consumers' privacy rights. As part of the settlement, Facebook also agreed to adopt new policies to better protect the privacy of its users. Facebook CEO Mark Zuckerberg announced a proposal to overhaul Facebook's privacy measures. The proposal included plans to use encrypted private messaging and make messages and stories impermanent. Later in 2019, Facebook announced a new tool called "Off-Facebook Activity." It allows users to see what personal information

In 2018, Mark Zuckerberg had to testify before the US Congress about Facebook's misuse of personal data. Zuckerberg promised that Facebook would improve its data privacy protections.

businesses, apps, and other groups are sharing with Facebook. The feature allows users to stop the tracking of their online activity and delete the data history from their accounts.

POLITICAL CAMPAIGNS AND DATA COLLECTION

While the Cambridge Analytica incident involved the illegal harvesting and selling of personal data, political campaigns often use freely available data to help promote their candidates. For many years, politicians have used voter information to help make their campaigns more effective.

But the prevalence of personal smartphone data has provided campaigns with a powerful additional tool. For example, at a 2018 rally for Beto O'Rourke, who was running against Texas senator Ted Cruz, a digital marketing company collected the unique identification (ID) numbers of smartphones that sent their location during the event. The company was able to match some of those ID numbers with contact information and compile a list of likely O'Rourke supporters. Just as data is used to target ads at likely buyers, campaign workers were able to follow up with the contacts, who were likely to vote for O'Rourke.

Data collection from apps is generally legal as long as the apps disclose that the information is being collected. Privacy policies usually explain that the data will be used for targeted advertising, but the policies may not reveal that the data could be used for political purposes. Kimberly Taylor is a Democratic political strategist. She was part of a group that tried to unseat Cruz in 2018. The group partnered with the software company Phunware to target people who went to political events in an effort to gain their support. She says, "People might get freaked out about this technology. But we're trying to use it for good, trying to engage more people in the [political] process."[25]

THE ROLE OF TECHNOLOGY COMPANIES

There is broad consensus over the need for better data privacy protections. But that consensus quickly breaks down over the question of who is responsible for helping to ensure that users' data is protected. Some people argue that smartphone users are making a purely voluntary decision in allowing their data to be collected. But other experts believe that devices and apps have become so sophisticated when it comes to data harvesting that it is virtually impossible for smartphone users to protect themselves.

Many people think the government and businesses involved in the collection and usage of data should play the biggest role in protecting users' privacy. Some tech company leaders have called for greater accountability among those in the industry. Apple CEO Tim Cook said, "We shouldn't sugarcoat the consequences. This is surveillance. And these stockpiles of personal data serve only to enrich the companies that collect them."[26]

CHAPTER FOUR

WHAT'S NEXT FOR SMARTPHONE PRIVACY?

With so many ways to access smartphone data and so many parties interested in collecting and using it, many smartphone users feel there is little point in trying to combat the system. However, there are steps users can take to help protect their private information. While it is not possible to completely stop apps and service providers from collecting and sharing personal data, it is possible for users to limit how much of their data is shared.

STEPS TO INCREASE PRIVACY PROTECTIONS

To start, there are some easy, fundamental steps all smartphone users can and should take to better protect their data. Passcode protection is the first basic step users

There are several easy ways to improve cell phone security. Setting up a passcode can help make data more private.

can take. Users can find this feature in the settings on their phone. The passcode can be a multi-digit number. Users should avoid obvious combinations such as 1234. Some smartphones also have fingerprint or facial recognition as a security option.

Mobile apps that contain personal data, such as banking or email accounts, should be password protected. Also, people should never use the same password for more than one account. If a hacker figures out one password, and more than one account has the same password, the hacker will be able to break into multiple accounts.

In many cases, apps will collect more data than they need. If it isn't clear why an app needs access to personal information, it is best to not give the app permission to collect this information. Georgia Weidman is the founder and CEO of Shevirah, a cybersecurity company. She explains, "If it's an app that lets you play cards, it probably doesn't need access to the inner workings of

HOW SECURE IS FACIAL RECOGNITION?

In 2017, Apple introduced Face ID as a way to unlock its latest smartphone, the iPhone X. Owners of this smartphone could use this method to unlock their phones instead of using the fingerprint sensor method from Apple's older iPhone models. Apple claimed Face ID was not only more convenient but also more secure than passcodes and the fingerprint sensor. This is certainly true in some cases. Many smartphone owners fail to lock their phones with a passcode due to the slight inconvenience of needing to enter it to unlock the phone. Unlocking a phone by just looking at it is easier and more efficient. But while Apple's Face ID system uses a sophisticated two-camera method to authenticate an owner's identity, not every smartphone that uses facial recognition is so secure. Dutch consumer protection organization Consumentenbond tested 110 smartphones that had facial recognition. They found that forty-two of these phones could be unlocked just by using a photo of the device's owner. Phones made by LG, Nokia, Samsung, BlackBerry, and Lenovo/Motorola all failed the security test.

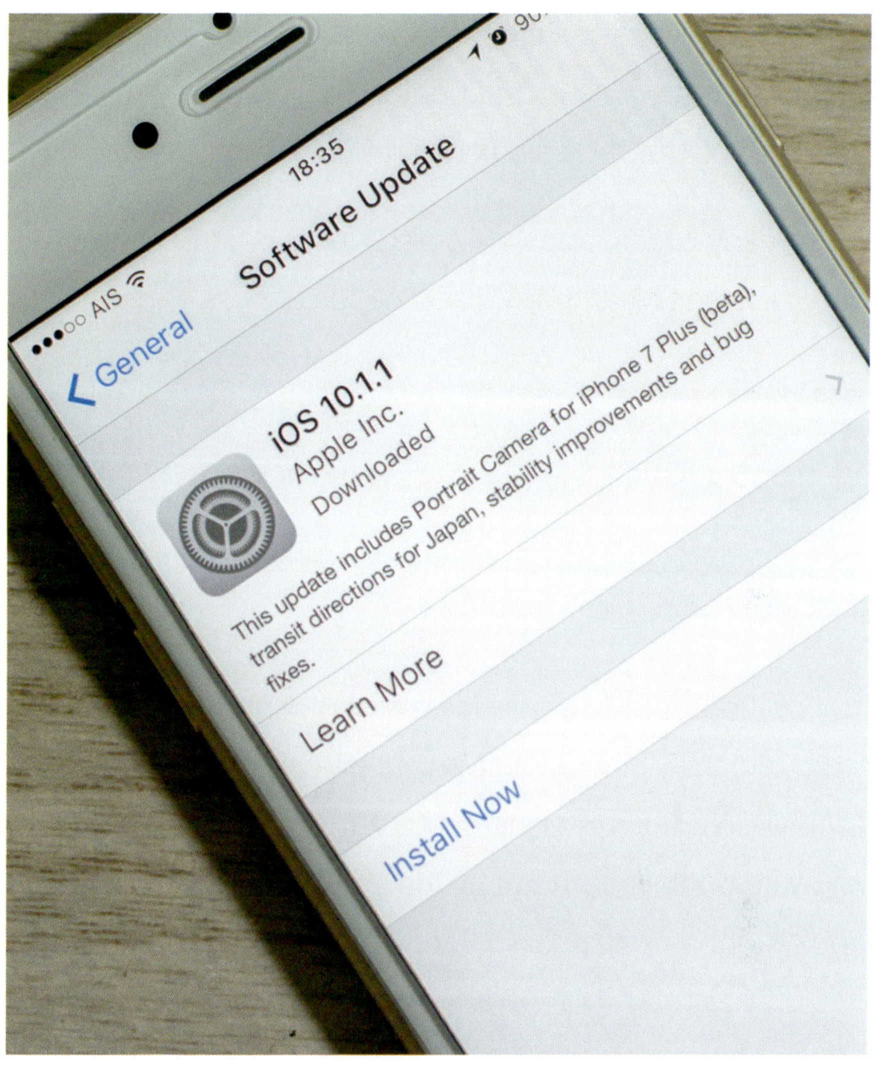

Updating phone operating systems is one action users can take to protect against cybercrime and other threats. However, a 2016 Pew Research Center survey found that 14 percent of smartphone users never update their phone's operating system.

your phone, your contact list, the internet and your GPS."[27] Users should be especially careful about giving apps access to their phone's camera, microphone, contact list, or location data.

Operating systems can help protect phone data from security threats. The most updated version of an operating system provides the best protection. New security threats can arise at any time, and when they are discovered, the phone companies develop patches to improve their phones' security. Patches are pieces of code designed to solve security problems or prevent newly discovered malware from infecting a device. If users do not do regular operating system updates, their data may be left unprotected. Then cybercriminals could gain access to valuable data, such as the users' financial information.

For those interested in doing more than the minimum to protect their privacy, antivirus apps can offer greater security. While many people routinely install antivirus software on their computers, the use of antivirus phone apps is not as widespread. Many of the same companies that offer antivirus software for computers also make smartphone antivirus apps. Antivirus apps provide security protections to prevent users from downloading files, such as apps and images, that have been infected with malware.

TWO-FACTOR AUTHENTICATION

Security experts also recommend that smartphone owners use two-factor authentication, especially for apps or online accounts that have particularly sensitive information.

Two-factor authentication is an extra layer of security. The user enters both a password and an additional code to log into an account. The code is sent either by text or by email. This security feature is especially helpful in cases when a user's password is stolen. Even if they have the password, hackers cannot gain access to an account without the additional code. Cybersecurity expert Bruce Schneier says, "Passwords are easy to steal, passwords are easy to guess. Use two-factor authentication. It's kind of a no-brainer."[28]

VIRTUAL PRIVATE NETWORKS

When people use public Wi-Fi, any information they send over the network may be vulnerable to theft. For this reason, security experts recommend that users never make any financial transactions while using a public Wi-Fi network. Many experts even caution against checking email or accessing social media while using public Wi-Fi because users may need to input passwords to access these accounts.

Smartphone owners can also use a virtual private network (VPN) to protect their data. A VPN is a subscription service. It creates a private network for a user while the user is on a public internet connection. A VPN makes an encrypted tunnel through which the user's internet traffic is routed, preventing the user's data from being accessed by others.

When choosing a VPN, it is important to exercise caution and choose a reputable service. People should research services carefully, relying only on trustworthy sources, before signing up. It is also important to read the VPN service agreement. At the very least, smartphone users should never choose a free VPN. Two independent investigations in 2018 found that 86 percent of the free VPN apps offered for iOS and Android operating systems had weak data protection policies. Data collected by the VPN services was shared with third parties. Some data was even shared with Chinese authorities. In contrast, media company CNET reviewed a sample of paid VPN services. It found that none of the top-rated services engaged in these questionable practices.

LIMITING LOCATION TRACKING

Among all the data collected from smartphones, user location data is some of the most widely gathered, used, and sold. Users can turn off location services in their phone's settings. This helps limit geotracking. However, many users do not realize that disabling this feature does

Even when location services are turned off, a phone's camera app still records location information. New operating systems may allow users to choose whether to share their location with an app on a case-by-case basis.

not completely prevent their location from being tracked.

Smartphones track users' location data in other ways too. For example, when someone takes a photo with a smartphone camera, the camera embeds GPS coordinates into the photo file itself. This information can be helpful for organizing photos by date or location. But it is another way potentially sensitive information is captured. When the user shares the photo, the embedded location data goes along with it. There is a way to keep this information private. The user can go to the camera app within the phone's settings to turn off this location sharing.

Most smartphone users are unaware that their phones keep a history of their movements, including how often they visit places such as stores. This feature is called "Significant Locations" on iPhones and "Location History" on Android phones. It can be found in the phone's settings and turned off.

RESPONSES FROM TECH COMPANIES

After years of paying relatively little attention to data privacy, 2019 became the year when the major tech companies tried to outdo each other in their calls for greater privacy protections. This development has come on the heels of some high-profile cases involving the misuse of personal data collected from various sources, including smartphone apps.

In an interview with ABC's Diane Sawyer in 2019, Apple's CEO Tim Cook announced, "We [at Apple] treasure your data. We want to help you keep it private and keep it secure. We're on your side."[29] Google's CEO Sundar Pichai wrote in an opinion piece for the *New York Times*, "Yes, we use data to make products more helpful for everyone. But we also protect your information."[30] In an obvious swipe at Apple, Pichai added, "Privacy cannot be a luxury good offered only to people who can afford to buy premium products and services."[31]

Microsoft CEO Satya Nadella spoke about data protection at the 2019 Mobile World Congress, the world's largest exhibition of electronic and telecommunications firms. He stated, "Data privacy is a human right. At Microsoft, we understand that we are the custodians of data which has been earned by the trust of the user."[32]

Even Zuckerberg joined the chorus of voices in support of greater privacy controls. At Facebook's 2019 annual developer conference, Zuckerberg said, "I know that we don't exactly have the strongest reputation on privacy right now, to put it lightly. But I'm committed to doing this well."[33]

In response to more demands for privacy protections, Google included a host of new privacy features in the

Tim Cook became the CEO of Apple in 2011. Cook and other tech leaders have promised to develop better security features for their devices and services.

Android 10 operating system, released in October 2019.

For example, Google added an auto-delete function to

location history, web and app activity, and YouTube search

history. Users can choose whether they would like this

activity data to be saved for three or eighteen months. The data will be automatically deleted after that time.

Apple added many new privacy features to its operating system in 2019. For instance, Apple gave users more options to limit the ability of apps to track their location. In the past, users had three options for app location tracking. They could opt to always share their location data with an app, only share the data while the app was in use, or never share the location data with the app. The new fourth option users could select was "Allow Once." If selected, the app will use the location data for the current task, but it will ask the user before using his or her location data again. The app will not be able to continue accessing location data when it is not in use. If "Always Allow" is selected, users will be periodically reminded about apps that are tracking their location.

GOVERNMENT PROTECTIONS

The increased attention to the improper collection and misuse of private data, spurred on by the Cambridge Analytica scandal in 2018, intensified calls for a federal privacy law in 2019. While some individual states have data privacy laws, many companies would prefer one comprehensive federal law rather than having to comply with an array of requirements that differ from state to state.

Věra Jourová, the vice president of the European Commission, shared information about the General Data Protection Regulation (GDPR) on May 25, 2018. The GDPR went into effect on that day.

In 2018, the EU enacted a law called the General Data Protection Regulation (GDPR). The GDPR standardized data protection laws across all EU countries. The law places strict rules on controlling and processing personally identifiable information. It requires that people give consent before their data can be collected and that their data must remain anonymous. Companies must notify customers if they experience a data breach and personal data is stolen from their computer systems. The GDPR also significantly increased penalties and fines for any violations of data privacy laws. Many people think the GDPR could be a model for possible US federal legislation.

While several privacy bills were introduced in the United States in 2019, Republican and Democratic members of Congress failed to meet a compromise on these bills. Congress members are still discussing these bills. During a Senate hearing on a potential federal privacy law, Republican senator Marsha Blackburn said, "We want to do something that is correct the first time around."[34]

One privacy bill that was introduced in Congress in 2019 is called the Privacy Bill of Rights Act. If this bill is passed into law, it would provide the most comprehensive set of privacy controls in the United States. Democratic senator Edward Markey, who created the bill, took provisions from the GDPR and the CCPA. The bill would require companies to obtain consent from people before collecting or using their personal information. Companies would also need

to allow people to access, correct, delete, or transfer any
information collected about them.

Another bill that was introduced in 2019 would create
a Digital Privacy Agency. This federal agency would be
charged with enforcing people's tech privacy rights. It would
also provide people with more control over how online
services make use of their personal data.

LOOKING AHEAD

The most important step smartphone users can take
toward protecting their privacy is to become aware of the
risks surrounding the use of their phones. It is important to
know what information is being collected, who is collecting
it, and what is happening to it. Bob Sullivan, a technology
correspondent with MSNBC, summed up the general
public's attitude toward privacy. He said, "Privacy does
matter—at least sometimes. But it's like health: When you
have it, you don't notice it. Only when it's gone do you wish
you'd done more to protect it."[35]

In addition, privacy
advocates believe people
should ask for more
transparency from tech
companies that are
involved in the collection

and distribution of private data. People can demand better protections from these companies. Government leaders can continue to work toward passing laws that create more controls over how private data is handled.

There is no one clear answer for how to best address the loss of privacy that arose from technological advances, including the creation of the smartphone. Smartphones have become an essential part of society. Every day, people depend on smartphones to perform basic tasks and help them navigate through life. One major trade-off for the convenience and services smartphones provide is the loss of control users have over their personal data. However, people can take more personal responsibility to protect their data by learning about the tools and options that are available to help them preserve their privacy. Governments can impose limits on what is allowed and not allowed. If privacy is indeed a human right, as many experts and people around the world consider it to be, advocates believe it deserves to be respected and not taken for granted.

SOURCE NOTES

INTRODUCTION: PRIVACY CHALLENGES IN THE SMARTPHONE AGE

1. Quoted in Jennifer Valentino-DeVries et al., "Your Apps Know Where You Were Last Night, and They're Not Keeping It Secret," *New York Times*, December 10, 2018. www.nytimes.com.

2. Quoted in Molly Callahan, "What We've Gained—and Lost—after a Decade with Smartphones," *News@Northeastern*, September 13, 2017. http://news.northeastern.edu.

3. Lorraine Courtney, "Lorraine Courtney: 'Our Data Is Being Used to Manipulate and Control Us—So Where Is the Outrage?'" *Independent.ie*, September 6, 2019. www.independent.ie.

4. Quoted in Richard Nieva, "At F8, Zuckerberg Unveils Facebook's New Mantra: 'The Future Is Private,'" *CNET*, April 30, 2019. www.cnet.com.

CHAPTER 1: WHAT ARE THE PRIVACY CONCERNS REGARDING SMARTPHONES?

5. Quoted in David Petersson, "What Companies Do With Your Personal Data And How Blockchain Protects It," *Forbes*, October 31, 2018. www.forbes.com.

6. Quoted in Rob Price and Mary Meisenzahl, "The First iPhone Was Announced 13 Years Ago Today—Here's How Steve Jobs Introduced It," *Business Insider*, January 9, 2020. www.businessinsider.com.

7. Quoted in Arkady Yerukhimovich et al., "Can Smartphones and Privacy Coexist?" *RAND Corporation*, 2016. www.rand.org.

8. Quoted in Mike Gikas, "How to Protect Your Privacy on Your Smartphone," *Consumer Reports*, February 1, 2017, www.consumerreports.org.

9. Shelby Brown, "7 Security Tips to Keep People and Apps from Stealing Your Data," *CNET*, July 10, 2019. www.cnet.com.

10. Quoted in Janna Anderson and Lee Rainie, "Concerns about the Future of People's Well-Being," *Pew Research Center*, April 17, 2018. www.pewresearch.org.

11. Katharine Schwab, "I Tried to Understand Location Tracking. It's Nearly Impossible," *Fast Company*, March 20, 2019. www.fastcompany.com.

CHAPTER 2: HOW DOES SMARTPHONE PRIVACY AFFECT INDIVIDUALS?

12. Quoted in Nicole Lindsay, "The Privacy Paradox Could Determine the Next Evolution of Privacy Regulation," *CPO Magazine*, November 30, 2018. www.cpomagazine.com.

13. Quoted in David Berreby, "Click to Agree with What? No One Reads Terms of Service, Studies Confirm," *Guardian*, March 3, 2017. www.theguardian.com.

14. Quoted in Maria Temming, "Smartphones Put Your Privacy at Risk," *Science News for Students*, January 30, 2018. www.sciencenewsforstudents.org.

15. Quoted in Lily Hay Newman, "Mobile Websites Can Tap Into Your Phone's Sensors Without Asking," *Wired*, September 26, 2018. www.wired.com.

16. J.D. Biersdorfer, "The Security of Cellular Connections," *New York Times*, August 10, 2018. www.nytimes.com.

17. Quoted in Jason Morris and Ed Lavandera, "Why Big Companies Buy, Sell Your Data," *CNN*, August 23, 2012. www.cnn.com.

18. Michael Grothaus, "Cheap Smartphones Have a Disturbing Secret," *Fast Company*, October 3, 2019. www.fastcompany.com.

SOURCE NOTES CONTINUED

CHAPTER 3: HOW DOES SMARTPHONE PRIVACY AFFECT SOCIETIES?

19. Quoted in Thomas Germain, "The Right to Remain Private: Where U.S. Law Lets You Down," *Consumer Reports*, August 29, 2019. www.consumerreports.org.

20. Quoted in Germain, "The Right to Remain Private: Where U.S. Law Lets You Down."

21. Quoted in Arjun Kharpal, "Order to Hack iPhone for FBI 'Chilling': Tim Cook," *CNBC*, February 17, 2016. www.cnbc.com.

22. Quoted in Arjun Kharpal, "Apple vs FBI: All You Need to Know," *CNBC*, March 29, 2016. www.cnbc.com.

23. Orin Kerr, "Supreme Court Agrees to Hear 'Carpenter v. United States,' the Fourth Amendment Historical Cell-Site Case," *Washington Post,* June 5, 2017. www.washingtonpost.com.

24. Quoted in Amy Davidson Sorkin, "In Carpenter, the Supreme Court Rules, Narrowly, for Privacy," *New Yorker*, June 22, 2018. www.newyorker.com.

25. Quoted in Sam Schechner, Emily Glazer, and Patience Haggin, "Political Campaigns Know Where You've Been. They're Tracking Your Phone," *Wall Street Journal*, October 10, 2019. www.wsj.com.

26. Quoted in Sara Salinas and Sam Meredith, "Tim Cook: Personal Data Collection Is Being 'Weaponized Against Us with Military Efficiency,'" *CNBC*, October 24, 2018. www.cnbc.com.

CHAPTER 4: WHAT'S NEXT FOR SMARTPHONE PRIVACY?

27. Quoted in Catherine Stupp, "Tips for Keeping Your Mobile Phone (Relatively) Safe," *Wall Street Journal*, September 18, 2019. www.wsj.com.

28. Quoted in Stupp, "Tips for Keeping Your Mobile Phone (Relatively) Safe."

29. Quoted in Allie Yang and Tess Scott, "Apple CEO Tim Cook Talks Protecting Customers' Private Data, Limiting Screen Time: 'You are Not Our Product,'" *ABC News*, May 3, 2019. https://abcnews.go.com.

30. Sundar Pichai, "Google's Sundar Pichai: Privacy Should Not Be a Luxury Good," *New York Times*, May 7, 2019. www.nytimes.com.

31. Pichai, "Google's Sundar Pichai: Privacy Should Not Be a Luxury Good."

32. Quoted in Rohan Abraham, "Microsoft CEO Satya Nadella Wants to Keep User Data Safe, Calls It a 'Human Right,'" *Economic Times*, February 20, 2019. https://economictimes.indiatimes.com.

33. Quoted in Julia Carrie Wong, "Facebook's Zuckerberg Announces Privacy Overhaul: 'We Don't Have the Strongest Reputation,'" *Guardian*, April 30, 2019. www.theguardian.com.

34. Quoted in Tim Peterson, "'Privacy Horse Is Sort of Out of the Barn': Congress Circles Closer to Federal Privacy Law," *Digiday*, May 22, 2019. www.digiday.com.

35. Bob Sullivan, "Privacy under Attack, but Does Anybody Care?" *NBC News*, October 17, 2006. www.nbcnews.com.

FOR FURTHER RESEARCH

BOOKS

Melissa Abramovitz, *Online Predators*. San Diego, CA: ReferencePoint Press, 2017.

Jamuna Carroll, *Thinking Critically: Cybercrime*. San Diego, CA: ReferencePoint Press, 2019.

Kathryn Hulick, *Protecting Financial Data*. Minneapolis, MN: Abdo Publishing, 2020.

Patricia D. Netzley, *Cell Phones: Threats to Privacy and Security*. San Diego, CA: ReferencePoint Press, 2015.

Laura Perdew, *Online Identity*. Minneapolis, MN: Abdo Publishing, 2017.

INTERNET SOURCES

Mona Bushnell, "10 Ways to Secure Your Smartphone Against Hackers," *Business News Daily*, June 7, 2019. www.businessnewsdaily.com.

Charlotte Empey, "9 Smartphone Tips Everyone Forgets to Follow," *Avast* (blog), November 1, 2019. https://blog.avast.com.

Louise Matsakis, "The WIRED Guide to Your Personal Data (and Who Is Using It)," *Wired*, February 15, 2019. www.wired.com.

"Smartphone Privacy," *Privacy Rights Clearinghouse*, December 19, 2017. www.privacyrights.org.

Jennifer Valentino-DeVries et al., "Your Apps Know Where You Were Last Night, and They're Not Keeping It Secret," *New York Times*, December 10, 2018. www.nytimes.com.

WEBSITES

Consumer Reports
www.consumerreports.org

Consumer Reports helps people learn more about data protection
and digital security. It also provides tips on how to protect data.

National Public Radio: Technology
www.npr.org/sections/technology

National Public Radio offers news stories about the latest technology
issues and their effects on society.

New York Times: The Privacy Project
www.nytimes.com/series/new-york-times-privacy-project

The *New York Times* offers a series of articles about the challenges of
protecting privacy in a technology-driven world.

INDEX

INDEX CONTINUED

IMAGE CREDITS

Cover: © Georgejmclittle/Shutterstock Images

5: © Rawpixel.com/Shutterstock Images

7: © antb/Shutterstock Images

8: © Sushiman/iStockphoto

11: © Monkey Business Images/Shutterstock Images

12: © faungfupix/Shutterstock Images

15: © Red Line Editorial

18: © Jacob Lund/Shutterstock Images

21: © photobyphm/Shutterstock Images

24: © Lenscap Photography/Shutterstock Images

27: © ViewApart/iStockphoto

30: © alvarez/iStockphoto

34: © Cristian Dina/Shutterstock Images

38: © mangpor_2004/iStockphoto

41: © Daniel J. Macy/Shutterstock Images

47: © Lowe Llaguno/Shutterstock Images

48: © EQRoy/Shutterstock Images

51: © Frederic Legrand - COMEO/Shutterstock Images

55: © Wachiwit/iStockphoto

57: © Photo_PG/Shutterstock Images

61: © Kryuchka Yaroslav/Shutterstock Images

64: © John Gress Media Inc/Shutterstock Images

66: © Alexandros Michailidis/Shutterstock Images

ABOUT THE AUTHOR

Carol Kim is the author of several fiction and nonfiction books for children. She has written about topics ranging from current issues and their effects on society to fun tales featuring the adventures of kids and animals alike. She loves exploring the world in person and through books. She lives with her family in Austin, Texas.